LOVE'S RESILIENCE: A STORY OF TWO SOULS

PRANAV SURISETTY

Made with ♥ on the Notion Press Platform
www.notionpress.com

Contents

Foreword

When I first read "Love's Resilience: A Story of Two Souls," I was immediately struck by the honesty and vulnerability with which the author tells their love story. It is a story that is all too familiar, yet it is also unique and deeply personal.

The author's journey through love and life is one that is relatable to many of us. It is a story of resilience and perseverance, of growth and self-discovery. It is a story of two souls coming together to create something beautiful and lasting.

As I read this book, I was reminded of my own journey through love and life. I was reminded of the importance of communication, trust, and taking risks. I was reminded of the beauty and strength of my own love story.

I believe that this book will resonate with readers of all ages and backgrounds. It is a story that will inspire you to reflect on your own journey, and to see the beauty and strength in your own love story.

So, turn the page, and join the author on their journey of love, growth, adventure and self-discovery.

Preface

When I first sat down to write this book, I had no idea where the journey would take me. I knew that I wanted to tell the story of my love with Emily, but I had no idea how much it would mean to me. As I wrote, I found myself reflecting on the journey that we had been on together, and I was amazed at how much we had grown and changed as individuals and as a couple.

This book is not just a love story, but it is a story of growth, adventure and self-discovery. It is a story of two souls coming together to create something beautiful and lasting. It is a story of resilience and perseverance, and of the power of love to overcome any obstacle.

I hope that as you read this book, you will be inspired to reflect on your own journey and to see the beauty and strength in your own love story. I hope that you will learn something new about yourself and about the power of love, and that you will be reminded of the importance of communication, trust, and taking risks.

So, turn the page, and join me on the journey of a lifetime.

- Pranav Surisetty

Acknowledgements

Writing this book has been a fantasy journey of a lifetime, and I could not have done it without the support and encouragement of the people in my life.

First and foremost, I would like to thank my imagination partner, Emily, for being my rock, my inspiration and my love. Without you, this book would not have been possible. I am forever grateful for your unwavering support and love.

I would also like to thank my family and friends, who have been with me through the ups and downs of this journey. Your love and support has meant the world to me.

I would like to extend my gratitude to my editor, [editor's name], for guiding me through the editing process and helping me to shape my thoughts into a coherent narrative.

Finally, I would like to thank my readers, for taking the time to read my story and for sharing in this journey with me. Your support and encouragement has been invaluable.

Thank you, thank you, thank you.

Prologue

As I sit down to write the story of my love with Emily, I realize that it has been a journey of a lifetime. From the moment we first met, to the moment we said "I do," and all the way through to the present day, our lives have been intertwined in the most beautiful and unexpected ways.

When I first laid eyes on Emily, I knew there was something special about her. She was different from anyone I had ever met before, and I couldn't help but feel a pull towards her. But, as fate would have it, the timing was not right and we went our separate ways.

Years passed, and our paths crossed again. We were older, wiser and ready for something new. We both knew that we had something special, and we were determined to make it work.

But, as with any great love story, our journey was not without its challenges. We had to learn to communicate and trust each other, to prioritize our relationship and to navigate the ups and downs of life together.

Through it all, we never gave up on each other. We fought for our love, and we came out stronger because of it. And, as we look back on our journey together, we realize that it has been one of the greatest adventures of our lives.

As I sit down to write this story, I realize that it is not just about me and Emily, but it's about the power of love and the strength of the human spirit. It's about the importance of communication, trust and taking risks. It's about the beauty of growth and self-discovery.

So, as you turn the pages of this love story, know that it is not just about two people, but it's about the journey of two souls coming together to create something beautiful and lasting.

"Love is not always easy,

but it is worth fighting for."

1

The First Glance

It all started with a simple glance. We were both working at the same company, and our paths crossed in the office from time to time. But there was nothing more to it. No jolt of electricity, no sweat on the palms, no knots in my stomach. Just a simple glance and then we'd go about our business.

As time passed, those occasional glances turned into more frequent ones. We started to notice each other more and more. I couldn't help but admire her cool, composed demeanor. She was always calm and collected, even in the most stressful of situations.

It was like she was immune to the chaos of the office. She was the kind of person who always seemed to have everything under control, and I couldn't help but be drawn to that.

Weeks turned into months, and before I knew it, we had been glancing at each other for quite some time. It's funny how time can fly by when you're not paying attention. But in the grand scheme of things, a couple of months isn't all that long. Unless, of course, you're in a suffocating conference room. Then, time seems to stand still.

But as I said, I couldn't help but admire her. Her calm and comfortable presence was like a breath of fresh air in the stuffy office. And without even realizing it, I found myself becoming attracted to her. I was drawn to her, and the more I saw her, the more I admired her.

It was then that the question popped into my head: Could it be love? I couldn't believe that I was even entertaining such a thought. After all, we had only ever exchanged glances. But still, the question lingered.

I didn't know what to do with these feelings, so I decided to start the staring game. I would glance at her discreetly, but in a way that she would know I was looking at her. But she didn't seem to mind. In fact, she didn't seem to be bothered at all. My ego was crushed. I thought that maybe she didn't feel the same way, and I was embarrassed to have even tried.

Feeling embarrassed and defeated, I decided to stop staring at her. But a few days later, I noticed that she was searching for me, looking for my glances. Little did I know, my glances had made her fall in love with me. She had been too shy to confess her feelings before, but my glances had given her the courage to do so.

Once I found out, I couldn't believe it. I had been too busy wallowing in my own embarrassment to notice that she had been falling for me the whole time. We started dating, and everything seemed perfect. We were both on the same page, and we were happy.

But as with all relationships, we faced our share of struggles. We had to navigate the challenges of long distance and the pressures of daily life. But through it all, we stuck together and our love only grew stronger.

Eventually, we were able to be together permanently and our love story had a happy ending. We were like two puzzle pieces that fit together perfectly. Our love had started with nothing more than a simple glance, but it was enough to change our lives forever.

Looking back on that time, I realize that love can come from the most unexpected places. You never know when or where you're going to meet that special someone. But when you do, it's like the universe conspires to bring you together. And that's exactly what happened with us. Our love story began with a simple glance, but it was enough to change our lives forever

2

The Attraction

As I continued to admire her from afar, my feelings for her grew stronger and more complex. I couldn't shake off the thought that there was something special about her and that I was meant to be with her. I found myself daydreaming about her, imagining scenarios where we would finally talk and get to know each other.

I was always on the lookout for opportunities to catch her gaze, and when our eyes finally met, my heart would race with excitement. I knew that I was falling for her, and it scared me. I had never felt this way before and I wasn't sure if she felt the same way.

I wanted to tell her how I felt, but I was too afraid of rejection. So, I decided to take a more subtle approach and try to be her friend first. I started making small talk with her whenever I saw her in the office, trying to get to know her better.

I found out that her name was Emily and that she loved reading, just like me. I also learned that she was a very kind and compassionate person.

As we spent more time together, I couldn't help but notice how she lit up whenever we talked. I was starting to believe that there was a chance for us, and that thought gave me the courage to ask her out on a date.

To my surprise, she said yes and we set a date for the following week. I was ecstatic, and I couldn't wait for the day to come. I spent the whole week counting down the minutes until our date.

The day finally arrived, and I was a bundle of nerves. I put on my best outfit, and headed to the restaurant where we had agreed to meet. When I saw her walk in, my heart skipped a beat. She looked stunning, and I couldn't believe that she was there with me.

The date was perfect. We talked and laughed, and it felt like we had known each other for years. I couldn't believe how natural it felt to be with her. As the night came to an end, I knew that I wanted to spend the rest of my life with her.

From that moment on, we were inseparable. We spent all our free ti

3

The Staring Game

As our relationship blossomed, I found myself constantly glancing at her, trying to catch her gaze. It was a game that we both played, and it brought us closer together. I couldn't get enough of her, and I wanted to be by her side every moment.

But as time went on, our glances started to take on a different meaning. They weren't just about attraction and infatuation anymore, but about the deep love and connection we shared. Every time our eyes met, it was like a silent conversation, filled with unspoken words of love and devotion.

I would find myself staring at her during meetings, while she was working on her computer, and even when she was asleep. I couldn't help it; I was mesmerized by her beauty and grace. And even though she would sometimes catch me staring, she never seemed to mind. In fact, she would often smile and give me a knowing look, as if to say that she felt the same way.

But as much as I loved staring at her, there were moments when it became too much. I would find myself getting lost in my thoughts, and it would take me out of the present moment. I realized that I needed to be more mindful and present, not just in my relationship but in my life as well.

So, I started to practice being more present and aware of my surroundings. I would take deep breaths and focus on the present moment, rather than getting lost in my thoughts about her. And as I did, I found that my love for her grew even deeper.

I also started to use my glances as a way to communicate with her, rather than just admiring her from afar. I would use them to express my love and affection, and to let her know that she was always on my mind.

We also started to play.

4

The Realization

As our relationship progressed, I started to realize that my love for Emily was not just a passing infatuation, but something deeper and more meaningful. I was truly in love with her, and I couldn't imagine my life without her.

But as much as I loved her, I also knew that our relationship was not without its challenges. We both had busy careers, and it was difficult to find time for each other. We also had different interests, and it was hard to find activities that we both enjoyed.

Despite these challenges, I knew that I wanted to spend the rest of my life with her. I wanted to make a commitment to her and our relationship. I wanted to show her how much she meant to me.

So, I decided to take the next step and talk to her about our future together. I knew it was a big step, but I was ready for it.

When I finally mustered up the courage to bring up the topic, I was surprised by her reaction. She told me that she had been feeling the same way, and that she also wanted to take our relationship to the next level.

We both agreed that we wanted to spend the rest of our lives together, and we decided to take the next step and move in together. It was a big decision, but we were both ready for it.

Moving in together was a big adjustment, but it brought us even closer together. We were able to spend more time together, and we were able to work through our challenges as a team.

As we settled into our new life, we faced new challenges. We had to learn how to live together, how to cook and clean, and how to share our space. It was not always easy, but we were determined to make it work.

One of the biggest challenges we faced was the fact that I was transferred to another department in the company and we had to work in different locations. This meant that we would see each other less, and it put a strain on our relationship. We were forced to rely on phone calls and video chats to stay in touch, and it was hard to maintain the intimacy that we had built.

But we were determined to make it work. We made a point to schedule regular dates, even if it meant traveling to see each other. We also made an effort to keep our communication open, and to be honest and transparent with each other.

As time went on, we realized that our love was strong enough to withstand the distance. We were able to maintain our connection, and we even grew closer as a result.

But just as we were starting to feel comfortable in our new arrangement, something unexpected happened. Emily started to look for me, wondering if I still stared at her like I used to. Little did I know, the staring game that we had played had made her fall in love with me.

It was a shock to realize that all this time she had feelings for me too, and I had missed it. But it also filled me with hope and joy, knowing that our love was mutual.

It was a realization that our love story was not just a coincidence, but it was meant to be. And it was a reminder that sometimes, it's the little things that make the biggest impact in our lives.

5

The Proposal

As Emily and I continued to grow closer, I knew that there was no one else in the world I wanted to spend the rest of my life with. I had never been happier and I was ready to take the next step in our relationship. I knew that it was time to propose to her.

I wanted to make the proposal special and meaningful, so I decided to put a lot of thought into it. I wanted to make sure that it was a moment that she would never forget.

First, I talked to her family and friends to ask for their blessing. I wanted to make sure that they were supportive of our relationship and that they would be happy for us.

Next, I started planning the perfect proposal. I decided to take her to the place where we had our first date. It was a small Italian restaurant in the city, and it held a special meaning for us both.

I made reservations for the same table where we sat on our first date and I made sure that the restaurant was decorated with candles and flowers. I also arranged for a pianist to play her favorite songs during dinner.

When the day of the proposal finally arrived, I was a bundle of nerves. I was excited and scared at the same time. But as soon as I saw her, all of my nerves dissipated. She looked beautiful and happy, and I knew that I was making the right decision.

During dinner, I couldn't take my eyes off of her. I was so in love with her, and I couldn't wait to spend the rest of my life with her.

After dinner, I led her to the table where we sat on our first date, and I got down on one knee. I looked into her eyes, and I told her how much I loved her and how much I wanted to spend the rest of my life with her.

With tears in her eyes, she said yes.

It was a moment that we would never forget, and it was the start of our forever together.

As we started planning our wedding, we realized that our love story was not just a fairytale, but it was real and it was ours. And we were ready to start our new chapter as husband and wife.

6

The Wedding Planning

After the proposal, Emily and I were over the moon with excitement. We were officially engaged and we couldn't wait to start planning our wedding.

We knew that we wanted a small, intimate wedding with just our closest family and friends. We wanted it to be a reflection of us as a couple and to be a day filled with love, laughter, and memories that would last a lifetime.

We started by setting a date and venue. We decided on a summer wedding in a beautiful garden. The venue was surrounded by lush greenery and had a picturesque pond with a small waterfall. It was the perfect setting for our special day.

Next, we began planning the details of the wedding. We wanted it to be elegant and romantic, so we chose a soft color palette of blush pink and white. We also decided to incorporate elements of nature, such as flowers and greenery, into the decor.

One of the most important decisions we had to make was choosing our wedding party. We wanted to make sure that we had the right people standing by our side on our special day. We chose our siblings as our best man and maid of honor, and we also selected a few close friends to be our groomsmen and bridesmaids.

As we started to finalize the details of the wedding, we faced some challenges. One of the biggest challenges was our budget. We had to make some sacrifices and cut back on some of the things we had wanted, but we knew that the most important thing was to be together on our special day.

But what made it all worth it was the love and affection we shared throughout the planning process. Even in the midst of all the stress and chaos, we made sure to take time for each other. We would have date nights where we would talk about the wedding and our future together. We would hold hands and steal kisses when no one was looking. These small moments of affection kept us grounded and reminded us why we were getting married in the first place.

We also made sure to involve each other in the planning process. Emily helped me pick out my tuxedo and I helped her pick out her wedding dress. We made it

7

The Big Day

The day of our wedding finally arrived, and I couldn't believe that the moment we had been planning for was finally here. As I got ready, I felt a mix of emotions - excitement, nervousness, and love. I knew that I was about to marry the love of my life, and I couldn't wait to see her walk down the aisle.

Emily looked absolutely stunning in her wedding dress, and I couldn't take my eyes off of her as she walked towards me. I felt like the luckiest man in the world, and I knew that this was the beginning of our forever together.

The ceremony was filled with love and emotion, and it was a beautiful reflection of our relationship. We wrote our own vows, and I couldn't help but shed a tear as I promised to love and cherish her for the rest of my days.

The reception was a blast, filled with laughter, dancing, and joy. We had a great time celebrating with our family and friends, and we were surrounded by so much love and happiness.

As the night came to a close, we took a moment to step away from the party and steal a moment alone. We sat by the pond and looked up at the stars, and I knew that this was the happiest moment of my life.

We said our goodbyes and left for our honeymoon, and I couldn't wait to start this new chapter of our lives together. We were husband and wife, and nothing could ever tear us apart.

As we spent our first days as a married couple, we felt a deep sense of contentment and happiness. We knew that we had found our forever in each other, and we were excited to face the future together.

We knew that our love story was not just a fairytale, but it was real and it was ours. And we were ready to start the next chapter of our lives, hand in hand, forever and always.

8

The First Year of Marriage

The first year of marriage was a whirlwind of emotions for Emily and me. We were adjusting to our new roles as husband and wife and learning how to navigate the ups and downs of married life.

One of the biggest challenges we faced was balancing our careers and our relationship. We both had demanding jobs and it was hard to find time for each other. We had to learn how to communicate effectively and make an effort to prioritize our relationship.

Despite the challenges, we knew that our love was strong enough to overcome anything. We made a point to schedule regular date nights, even if it meant sacrificing some of our free time. We also made an effort to keep our communication open and to be honest and transparent with each other.

We also made sure to keep the romance alive in our relationship. We would surprise each other with small gestures of love and affection, such as leaving love notes for each other or cooking each other's favorite meals. These small acts of love reminded us of the spark that brought us together in the first place.

We also made an effort to keep the romance alive in our relationship. We would surprise each other with small gestures of love and affection, such as leaving love notes for each other or cooking each other's favorite meals. These small acts of love reminded us of the spark that brought us together in the first place.

The first year of marriage was also a time for growth and change. We faced many challenges together, but we also celebrated many milestones and accomplishments. We grew closer as a couple and we learned how to support each other through the good times and the bad.

As we looked back on our first year of marriage, we knew that our love story was not just a fairytale

9

The Struggle

As Emily and I entered into the second year of our marriage, we found ourselves facing a new set of challenges. We had been so focused on adjusting to married life and building a strong foundation for our relationship, that we didn't realize how much the stress of our careers had been affecting us.

We both had demanding jobs and were working long hours, and it started to take a toll on our relationship. We were both exhausted and stressed out, and we found ourselves arguing more and more. We were struggling to find time for each other and to connect on a deeper level.

We knew that we needed to make a change, but we didn't know where to start. We felt like we were at a crossroads and we were unsure of what the future held for our relationship.

We decided to take a break and go on a vacation together, to try and reconnect and rebuild our relationship. We chose a remote cabin in the mountains, where we could escape from the distractions of our everyday lives and focus on each other.

The vacation was just what we needed. We were able to disconnect from our busy lives and reconnect with each other. We spent our days hiking and exploring the beautiful nature around us, and our nights sitting by the fire, talking and laughing.

We realized that the stress of our careers had been affecting us more than we had realized, and that we needed to make a change.

We decided to make an effort to prioritize our relationship and to find a balance between our work and our personal lives.

We set boundaries and made a plan to make more time for each other. We scheduled regular date nights and made an effort to take breaks from our work to spend time together.

It wasn't easy, but we were determined to make it work. We knew that

10

The Renewal

Emily and I had made a commitment to each other to work on our relationship, and we were determined to make it work. As we continued to navigate the ups and downs of marriage, we found that our renewed effort to prioritize our relationship was paying off.

We started to see a positive change in our relationship. We were communicating better and were more understanding of each other's needs. We were making more time for each other and were finding ways to connect on a deeper level.

One of the things that helped us to reconnect was to start doing things together that we both enjoyed. We started a new hobby together, which was hiking and camping. We found that being in nature together helped us to relax and to forget about the stress of our everyday lives.

We also made an effort to be more romantic with each other. We would surprise each other with small gestures of love and affection, such as cooking each other's favorite meals or buying each other small gifts. These small acts of love reminded us of the spark that brought us together in the first place.

We also made an effort to be more open and honest with each other. We would talk about our feelings, our fears, and our hopes for the future. We found that being honest and transparent with each other helped us to build trust and to understand each other better.

As we looked back on the past year, we knew that our relationship had come a long way. We had been through some difficult times, but we had also celebrated many milestones and accomplishments. We had grown closer as a couple and we had learned how to support each other through the good times and the bad.

We knew that our love story was not just a fairytale, but it was real and it was ours. And we were ready to take on the next chapter of our lives together, hand in hand, forever and always.

11

The New Beginning

As Emily and I entered into the third year of our marriage, we found ourselves facing a new set of challenges. We had been so focused on rebuilding our relationship and finding balance in our lives, that we didn't realize how much the stress of our careers had been affecting us in the long run.

We both realized that we needed to make a change in our careers in order to be truly happy and fulfilled. After much discussion and soul searching, we decided to take the leap and make a career change.

Emily decided to leave her job as a lawyer and pursue her dream of opening up her own bakery. She had always loved baking and had a passion for it. She had been thinking about this for a while, but she was scared to take the leap. With my support, she finally decided to take the risk and start her own business.

As for me, I decided to leave my job as an engineer and pursue my dream of becoming a writer. I had always loved writing and had a passion for it. I had been thinking about this for a while, but I was scared to take the leap. With Emily's support, I finally decided to take the risk and start my own writing career.

We knew that it wasn't going to be easy, but we were determined to make it work. We supported each other through the process of starting our own businesses, and we found that working together made it even more special.

The first few months were tough, but we were determined to make it work. We faced many challenges and obstacles, but we were able to overcome them with each other's support.

As our businesses started to take off, we felt a sense of fulfillment and happiness that we had never felt before. We were finally doing what we loved and were able to balance our careers and our personal lives.

We knew that our love story was not just a fairytale, but it was real and it was ours. And we were ready to take on the next chapter of our lives together, hand in hand, forever and always.

12

The Growth

As Emily and I continued to grow in our new careers, we also found ourselves growing as a couple. We had been through so much together and had come out stronger for it. We had learned how to support each other and how to navigate the ups and downs of life together.

We also found that our new careers had brought us closer together. We were able to share our passions and interests with each other, and we were able to understand each other's struggles and triumphs on a deeper level.

We also found that our businesses had allowed us to travel more and explore new places together. We took advantage of this opportunity and traveled to different parts of the world, experiencing new cultures and making memories that would last a lifetime.

As we looked back on the past few years, we realized that our love story was not just a fairytale, but it was real and it was ours. We had been through so much together and had come out stronger for it. We had learned how to support each other and how to navigate the ups and downs of life together.

We also found that our new careers had brought us closer together. We were able to share our passions and interests with each other, and we were able to understand each other's struggles and triumphs on a deeper level.

We also found that our businesses had allowed us to travel more and explore new places together. We took advantage of this opportunity and traveled to different parts of the world, experiencing new cultures and making memories that would last a lifetime.

As we looked back on the past few years, we realized that our love story was not just a fairytale, but it was real and it was ours. We had been through so much together and had come out stronger for it. We had learned how to support each other and how to navigate the ups and downs of life together.

We knew that our love story was not just a fairytale, but it was real and it was ours. And we were ready to take on the next chapter of our lives together, hand in hand, forever and always.

13

The Challenge

As Emily and I continued to navigate the ups and downs of life and marriage, we found ourselves facing a new challenge. We had been so focused on growing our careers and our relationship, that we didn't realize how much the stress of our busy lives had been affecting us.

We started to feel burnt out and overwhelmed, and we found ourselves arguing more and more. We were struggling to find time for each other and to connect on a deeper level. We realized that we needed to take a step back and re-evaluate our priorities.

We decided to take a break and go on a retreat together, to try and reconnect and rebuild our relationship. We chose a remote cabin in the mountains, where we could escape from the distractions of our everyday lives and focus on each other.

The retreat was just what we needed. We were able to disconnect from our busy lives and reconnect with each other. We spent our days hiking and exploring the beautiful nature around us, and our nights sitting by the fire, talking and laughing.

We realized that we had been so focused on achieving our goals and building our careers, that we had forgotten to take care of ourselves and our relationship. We decided to make a change and to prioritize our relationship and our well-being.

We set boundaries and made a plan to make more time for each other. We scheduled regular date nights and made an effort to take breaks from our work to spend time together. We also made an effort to take care of ourselves, by exercising, meditating, and taking time for self-care.

It wasn't easy, but we were determined to make it work. We knew that our love story was not just a fairytale, but it was real and it was ours. And we were ready to take on this new challenge together, hand in hand, forever and always.

14

The Adventure

As Emily and I continued to navigate the ups and downs of life and marriage, we found ourselves growing closer than ever before. We had learned to prioritize our relationship and our well-being, and we were reaping the benefits of it.

We decided to take our relationship to the next level by planning a trip of a lifetime together. We had always talked about traveling the world and experiencing new cultures, and we finally decided to make it happen.

We planned a year-long trip, visiting different countries and experiencing new cultures. We traveled to exotic places, such as the Amazon rainforest, the Great Wall of China, and the Pyramids of Egypt. We also visited more modern cities, such as Paris, Tokyo, and New York.

The trip was an adventure of a lifetime. We had the opportunity to experience new cultures, try new foods, and make new friends. We also had the opportunity to bond and make memories that would last a lifetime.

We also found that traveling together had brought us closer than ever before. We were able to share our passions and interests with each other, and we were able to understand each other's struggles and triumphs on a deeper level.

As we looked back on our trip, we realized that our love story was not just a fairytale, but it was real and it was ours. We had been through so much together and had come out stronger for it. We had learned how to support each other and how to navigate the ups and downs of life together.

We knew that our love story was not just a fairytale, but it was real and it was ours. And we were ready to take on the next chapter of our lives together, hand in hand, forever and always.

15

The End

As Emily and I looked back on our love story, we realized that it had been a journey of a lifetime. We had been through so much together, and we had come out stronger for it. We had learned how to support each other and how to navigate the ups and downs of life together.

We had experienced so many amazing things together, from the small moments of everyday life to the grand adventures of traveling the world. We had shared our passions and interests with each other, and we had made memories that would last a lifetime.

As we reflected on our journey together, we knew that our love story was not just a fairytale, but it was real and it was ours. We had been through so much together, and we had come out stronger for it. We had learned how to support each other and how to navigate the ups and downs of life together.

We knew that our love story was not just a fairytale, but it was real and it was ours. And we were ready to take on the next chapter of our lives together, hand in hand, forever and always.

We were grateful for the time we had spent together, the memories we had made and the love we shared. As we closed the book on our love story, we knew that it was not the end but the beginning of a new chapter in our lives. We were ready to face the future together, knowing that no matter what life throws at us, we would always have each other.

Epilogue

As I sit here, reflecting on my love story with Emily, I realize that it has been one of the greatest adventures of my life. From the moment I first laid eyes on her, to the moment we said "I do," and all the way through to the present day, my life has been a journey of love, growth and self-discovery.

Emily has been my rock, my guiding light and my partner in every sense of the word. Together, we have faced the highs and lows of life, and through it all, we have grown stronger as a couple.

We have learned that love is not always easy, but it is worth fighting for. We have learned that communication is key, and that it is important to prioritize our relationship and our well-being. We have learned that it is important to take risks and to pursue our passions, even if it means stepping out of our comfort zones.

As we look back on our journey together, we realize that it has been one of the greatest adventures of our lives. We have traveled the world, experienced new cultures and made memories that will last a lifetime. We have learned to support each other and to navigate the ups and downs of life together.

We have grown together, both as individuals and as a couple. We have learned to be honest and transparent with each other and to build trust. We have learned that love is not always easy, but it is worth fighting for.

As we close the book on our love story, we look forward to the future with hope and excitement. We know that there will be more challenges to come, but we also know that we will face them together, hand in hand, forever and always.

Love is not always easy but it is worth fighting for. My love story with Emily has been the greatest adventure of my life, and I am grateful for every moment we shared together. I know that our love story is not over yet, and I am excited for the next chapter of our lives together.

.

.

.

.

.

.

.

"Love is not just a feeling, it's a journey of resilience and perseverance."

Dear Reader's

Dear readers,

As you close the book on the story of my love with Emily, I hope that it has touched your heart and inspired you in some way. I hope that you have been able to relate to our story and that it has reminded you of the beauty and strength of your own love story.

I want to thank you for taking the time to read our story, and for joining us on this journey of growth, adventure and self-discovery. I hope that you have learned something new about yourself and about the power of love, and that you have been reminded of the importance of communication, trust, and taking risks.

I hope that this story has inspired you to reflect on your own journey and to see the beauty and strength in your own love story. I hope that it has reminded you of the importance of cherishing and fighting for the people you love.

Thank you for reading, and I hope our story has been able to touch you in some way.

Sincerely,

Pranav Surisetty.

Printed by Libri Plureos GmbH in Hamburg,
Germany